THE ALPHA'S PROTECTION

A PARANORMAL DADDY DOM BOOK

ALPHA DOMS

RENEE ROSE

RENEE ROSE ROMANCE

WANT FREE RENEE ROSE BOOKS?

Go to http://subscribepage.com/alphastemp to sign up for Renee Rose's newsletter and receive a free copy of *Alpha's Tempta-*

tion, Theirs to Protect, Owned by the Marine and more. In addition to the free stories, you will also get bonus epilogues, special pricing, exclusive previews and news of new releases.

FOREWORD

Dearest reader,

When the publishing rights to the *Alpha Doms* series returned to me from Stormy Night Publications, the original publisher, I considered a major re-edit / re-write, as I'd done with my *Made Men* series. It's been nearly ten years since *The Alpha's Hunger* was published, and my writing ability, style, and content have evolved significantly. I still love kink, but I've moved away from the punishy-style, keeping it more in the sexy realm.

In the end, I decided to leave the series as is—a picture in time. Humbling though it may be to me, by leaving it as is, you can see my evolution as a storyteller. *The Alpha's Hunger* (2015) is my billionaire boss wolf shifter 1.0., *Alpha's Temptation* (2017) became 2.0 and *Big Bad Boss* (2024) is 3.0. Who knows what shape 4.0 will take?

As always, I am eternally grateful to you, the reader, who keeps me writing, pushing my craft, and learning to find new depth with each story I tell. Thank you for your readership now, and if you've been with me since the beginning, a million kisses for sticking with me all this time.

THE ALPHA'S PROTECTION

by Renee Rose

Author's Note: The characters in this story have waited a very long time for their HEA. They were first introduced in my 2016 book, *The Alpha's Promise*. Because I knew Mark would be a daddy dom, the Dirty Daddies Anthology was a perfect opportunity for me to finally write their story and close out the *Alpha Doms* series.

Trigger warning: This book features a heroine who is on the run from an abusive ex. If such material triggers you, please skip this one!

Colleen

I strip off my clothes and dive into the moonlit swimming pool in the foothills of Denver.

My children and I were dropped here at the home of a total stranger—a wolf in the Denver pack—who pledged his protection of us the moment he met us. The reason he pledged it is no mystery.

I caught his scent, and my body came alive. I have to guess he experienced the same thing.

But we hardly spoke because he was involved in some kind of drug sting, and we were spirited away to the safety of his home until he returned.

The kidney-shaped pool is beautiful, with a natural oasis look and a waterfall into the hot tub at one end. There's a fall chill to the air, making steam rise from the warm water. The moon hangs low in a starry sky.

I swim the length of it underwater, emerging to fill my lungs. I haven't swum in years, but being in the water soothes away some of my frayed nerves.

I took my pups and ran away from my abusive mate in Kentucky just over a month ago, and every day, I regain a little more of myself. We're probably safe here, at least for the moment.

Even so, I'm swimming to burn off my anxiety. If Dirk—the asshole father of my pups—somehow finds us, there will be hell to pay. But I'm not going to let him drag us back, whatever he may threaten this time.

I can't go there. I have to believe he won't find us here—at least not tonight.

I dive back under the water and swim the full length of the pool again before emerging for air. When I do, I gasp.

The shifter's scent reaches me first—leather and coffee and delicious male. He's home.

DEA Agent Mark Ruhl stands at the edge of the pool staring down at me with a predatory gleam in his eyes. He's older than I am by at least ten years, maybe more, and he looks incredible in his uniform with broad shoulders and thick corded muscles running down his arms.

I bend my knees to hide my bare breasts under the water line, and our gazes lock.

"You don't have to be scared of me, little wolf." His voice is a rich baritone that sends tingles across my shoulders and the back of my neck. It rumbles deep with authority but not the kind I've learned to beware. The kind that inspires warmth and safety. Like the authority I thought my father wielded, before he arranged my mating to Dirk.

Mark crouches down, his eyes gleaming in the moonlight. He says nothing, just holds my gaze in a way that makes my heart pound. "Are you afraid?"

My body comes alive for the first time in years. My nipples pucker in the warm water, and frissons of heat warm my core. I swallow. "N-not of you," I admit.

His lips quirk a little at the corners. "Good. I'm sorry you were left here alone." The corners of his eyes crinkle. "I'm glad you're swimming. It looks like you felt safe."

I nod. "Did everything go all right with the drug bust?"

"Yes. Everything worked out."

I swirl my hands over the surface of the water, and my breasts cool as they come out. I immediately drop back down.

Mark's eyes take on a silver glow, and his nostrils flare. "Were you out here to tempt me, little she-wolf?"

I shake my head although now that he says it, I wonder if my she-wolf didn't orchestrate it.

"I think we both know that this attraction between us—" He stops speaking when I continue to shake my head, backing up.

"Okay. You're not ready to hear that. Of course you're not. Come back." He beckons to me, but I don't move. He shows no sign of irritation. Instead, he seems to soften. "You've been through a lot, Colleen—too much. I know you're still scared. I just want you to feel safe right now. To know that I'm going to take care of you and those pups. I won't let anyone touch you, I promise."

I believe him. I mean, I believe his intentions. But he doesn't know how powerful Dirk is—an alpha with a pack of at least 150 wolves. Nor how cruel.

And yes, I know Mark Ruhl is my true fated mate. I knew it the moment I caught his scent. Even now, my spirits lift being near him like the sun coming out after the storm from hell.

But I can't let him mark me and claim me as his own because doing so will sign the death warrant on both of us. Possibly my children, too. Dirk is that psychopathic and that powerful.

"Come here," he beckons again, and this time my body obeys of its own accord, creating minia-ture currents as I step forward to the edge of the pool.

He reaches for me, and I don't move out of his grasp, even though he's a near stranger and all I've known for the past ten years has been torment at the hands of a male. My body knows its master. My she-wolf wants to be claimed.

He shows off his shifter strength by plucking me out of the pool by my armpits like I'm a small child. Water drips from my naked body, but the cold doesn't touch me. Steam curls off the surface of my skin.

"I'm trying very hard not to look, sweetheart." His voice is pure gravel.

He sets me on my feet and then stoops to pick up the towel I left by the water's edge. He does look, though. His heated, hungry gaze rakes down my body as he wraps the terry cloth around me, a low growl sounding in his throat, his cock tenting the pants of his uniform.

I should be afraid. He may have trouble controlling his wolf, which means he may mark me against my consent. But I'm only hot and tingly for him. Restless and wanton.

He tucks in the edges of the towel above my breasts. His eyes glow completely silver—his wolf wants me.

I tremble, but still not with fear.

He hasn't let go of the towel, his fingers still tucked between my breasts, and he uses it to draw me closer. "I'm going to teach you to trust me," he murmurs, like he's swearing an oath. "I'm going to take care of your needs, babygirl. *All* your needs."

My breath puffs out of my lips on a soft note of shock, and I attempt to take a step backward, but he hangs onto the towel, keeping me close.

"Let me show you."

I shake my head jerkily. "I-I can't."

"I won't take from you. I just want to give, baby-girl." His nostrils flare as he breathes in my scent. "I can smell your need. Are you achy between those beautiful legs of yours, little wolf?" He slowly walks me backward.

I don't mean to answer him, but it's like I'm under a spell. Not the kind that makes a wolf's body physically respond to alpha dominance. Something deeper and more mysterious. My head wobbles in a *yes*.

My calves hit a chaise lounge and buckle. He holds me up with the towel.

"Let me kiss it better, Colleen. I need to taste you. Please, just a taste to get me through the night with you unclaimed."

I draw in a sharp breath. This wolf isn't backing off. But my body understands completely. My she-wolf is desperate for him. So I sit back, letting the towel fall open.

Mark doesn't wait two seconds before he's on his knees in front of the lounge, pushing my legs wide.

"*This pussy*," I hear him rumble although I have no idea what he means by it. It doesn't matter. He's licking into me, sending me into orbit with each expert swipe of his tongue. I've never experienced this before, and my eyes roll back in my head as every nerve ending comes alive.

He traces around my inner lips, penetrates me with the tip of his tongue. He pushes my knees up toward my shoulders and licks me from anus to clit.

It's intimate and embarrassing and incredibly pleasurable. I'm drunk on sensations, on his pheromones, on moonlight.

It's a first for me. Dirk never cared about my needs, and he is the only male I've known.

"This pussy," Mark repeats when he comes up for air.

"What about it?" I manage to choke out.

"So beautiful." He lowers his head again and flicks his tongue over my clit.

I run my fingers through his closely-shorn hair, arch my breasts toward the night sky. "Mark." My strangled cry sounds like it belongs to a different female. Certainly not to me.

"That's right, babygirl. Are you going to come all over Daddy's tongue?"

Did he call himself *Daddy*? My pussy gushes in response. It's so hot and wrong and embarrassing and *fates, yes*, I'm here for it.

"Come for Daddy."

My body responds immediately to the

command because my orgasm starts, curling my toes inward.

"Yes," I choke hoarsely as it deepens, my muscles squeezing and pulsing.

He slides two fingers inside me, and my walls seize around them as I let out a keening cry.

He sucks my clit while pumping his fingers and gets another orgasm out of me, this one so strong that my inner thighs squeeze around his shoulders, and my hips pop off the lounge.

I stare up at the stars as they spin and shift and rearrange. When the sky stops moving, my body falls limp, my breath slips in and out.

Mark rises above me, and I flinch because his eyes are still pure silver, and the bald hunger in his expression can only be for me. "Don't be afraid of me, babygirl. I told you I wouldn't take. I won't claim you until you're ready. Not until you ask me to. That's a promise."

"Mark," I murmur. It's a lament because I know how much pain he must be in to hold back.

My mate's hands shake as he reaches for the edges of my towel and carefully wraps it back around me. "Come here, beautiful." He uses the towel to smoothly lift me back to my feet. "Can you walk?"

I stare at him, dumbfounded. I've never had anyone take such care with me. It makes me want to weep. When I don't answer, he sweeps me up into his arms, picks up my clothes from the ground where I left them, and carries me inside.

The Denver pack alpha dropped us off this evening, opening the door with a code Mark had given him. He told us to make ourselves at home, but I didn't feel comfortable putting the kids in a bed until Mark was here to tell us where to go.

My pups are both asleep on couches in the living room, but Jayden, my nine-year-old, stirs at the sound of us coming in, and I stiffen.

Mark immediately lowers me to my feet, obviously understanding that I wouldn't want Jayden to see us that way.

The delirium of our stolen moment is gone, and the more familiar sense of urgency and fear creeps back in. I quickly yank on my clothes.

Mark picks up Angie, my six-year-old. She whimpers in her sleep, but her head falls heavy onto his shoulder. "I'll carry her upstairs," he tells me.

But there's no way Jayden would allow himself to be carried. His life has been as hard as mine has. I gently wake him. "Time to go to bed, buddy," I say quietly. "Come on."

He rolls swiftly to his feet, blinking and alert. My little warrior, always trying to protect me or his little sister.

On the way up the stairs, I catch sight of my reflection in a framed mirror and stop to stare. I look younger than I did yesterday—by at least five years. More my actual age. My skin, which had grown sallow and pale from the stress, glows in the lamplight. I touch the place in my mouth where I'm missing two teeth. Dirk knocked them out the day I left him, and they haven't grown back. My natural shifter healing abilities became suppressed as a result of the mental and emotional trauma he kept me in.

My gums ache now, and I feel the sharp edge of new teeth coming through.

I let out my breath in a puff of surprise. One orgasm was all it took.

One orgasm on the tongue of my mate, and I began to heal.

It seems too good to be true, but that's because it is.

I can't let Mark Ruhl claim me, no matter how he makes my body sing.

I would never endanger his life that way.

MARK

I don't ever want the taste of Colleen to leave my tongue. Satisfying my mate is my new mission in life. I don't know where that *daddy* thing came from —the kinky words just slipped from my lips as I was licking into her, but it felt right. As an alpha wolf, I've always been the dominant, but this is the first time I want to shelter and care for a woman. To spoil her and make sure she knows how cherished she is.

That she's mine. All mine.

But she's not ready for that... yet. Right now she's in survival mode, so I need to make her feel safe and protected.

I lead them upstairs and push open the door to the guest room. I don't turn on the light, so I don't disturb the sleeping pup. "The three of you can stay in this room, unless—"

"This will be fine," she says quickly, scooting past me to pull down the covers to the bed. I lay the little girl down in the middle, and she sighs and rolls over. The boy crawls in beside his sister and closes his eyes.

I'm not sure how I'll make it through the night with her unclaimed and under my roof, but I have to. She needs to feel safe.

I will clean out my office and turn it into a room for the kids right away, so they don't feel like guests in my house. I want them to know that this is their home now. To a human, it might seem nuts that I'm willing to rearrange my life for three people I just met, but for a wolf, there's no question. I've gone forty years thinking it unlikely I'd ever find my fated mate. I went to shifter games when I was in my twenties, as was expected, but when my alpha asked me to serve as a council enforcer, I stopped looking.

I go to the linen closet and pull out a stack of towels which I bring to Colleen. "The bathroom's right there. I think I have a few unopened toothbrushes in the top right drawer."

"Thank you." She doesn't look at me as she tucks the children into the bed.

She needs quiet and privacy, but I can't make myself leave the doorway. I want to pull her into my arms and soothe away the pinched worry that's returned to her face.

"Come here," I say softly. I don't mean to command it, but I have enough alpha in me that most everything comes out that way.

She slips past me to stand in the hallway. I leave the bedroom and shut the door.

"I can ask Cody to pack up your things in Colorado Springs," I offer in a low voice, so I don't wake the sleeping child. Cody is the alpha of the small pack there. Colleen had been living there and sought out his help yesterday after Jayden was hit by a car.

For a shifter, a car accident isn't the problem, it's having humans witness a spontaneous healing that would cause ripples. Cody had pulled them out of the hospital before Jayden was checked out and then took her to his place in case the hospital report triggered information being sent to her ex. I was in the Springs for the drug bust and met them there. Because Cody's pack would not be strong enough to fend off Colleen's former pack's larger numbers if they came for her, he requested help from the Denver pack, and I immediately volunteered my personal protection.

Colleen shakes her head. "We didn't have much there. Just a mattress and a few items of clothing."

I grind my teeth, horrified at the way my mate has been living. "I'll take you shopping tomorrow, then, for new clothes and toiletries. Whatever you need."

"Thank you." Her cinnamon scent fills my nostrils, agitating my wolf.

"Cody told me you require protection from your…" I can't make myself say the word *mate* because she belongs to me. But some other male has obviously claimed her. Multiple times and in brutal ways, judging by the unhealed scars on her shoulder. Something has affected her ability to heal—no doubt the stress of what she was living with.

"Our alpha," she supplies.

I try not to show my rage that any male deemed worthy of leading a pack would harm rather than protect those weaker than him.

"And you think he'll bring the whole pack when he comes?"

She shakes her head. "Maybe not. I didn't reach out to Cody until yesterday, when Jayden got hit by a car, and we had to go to a human hospital. I was afraid it would trigger some kind of notification if he'd filed a missing persons report."

"Right. I will check on that Monday when I go to work. I can access those kinds of records. But I don't want you to have to hide anymore, sweetheart. It would be better to put him on notice that you're here and under the Denver pack's protection."

"No," she says immediately.

A growl gets loose in my throat, making her flinch.

I reach out and touch her arm. "I'm sorry, babygirl. I'm not growling at you. I didn't mean to snarl."

She ducks her head to show submission in wolf fashion, and I want to punch my own face in.

"Can you tell me why you don't want to free yourself of him?"

She shakes her head. "I don't want a war between packs over me. I don't even know your pack, it's not fair to ask you to protect me."

I force down my primal need to tear her enemies apart limb by limb and lay them at her feet. I exhale slowly to get my violence under control. "It *is* fair to ask it," I say simply. I know she didn't want to hear me declare that she's my mate, so I don't say it now, but I'm certain she knows what I mean.

I can't decide if she doesn't believe me, doesn't

agree, or just isn't ready to contemplate a new mate, but for the moment, I need to be patient and take things slowly.

"There's something you should know about me," I say, hoping what I tell her doesn't spook her more.

She stiffens.

"I'm not just in human law enforcement. I'm an enforcer for the shifter council." Essentially, it means I have a gun with silver bullets and a license to kill. When shifters get on the wrong side of human law or if they become a danger to our species, the council may rule that a shifter must be put down. I'm the guy who carries out that justice. It's a secret role, for the protection of our families, much like the hooded executioner of medieval times. "It's a job I would quit the moment I have a mate." I slide a sideways glance at her to see how this landed. I need her to know that I wouldn't put our family at risk. But I also want her to understand I'm well-equipped to take care of trouble. "I just want you to know that if things get difficult, I can handle them."

She draws in a breath and lets it out slowly. "Good to know."

I allow myself a moment of relief that I didn't scare her more with my admission.

I cradle her face with one hand, my thumb brushing down her cheek. "You okay?"

She melts forward, almost leaning into me, but not quite. "Yes. Thank you." She keeps her gaze lowered in that old-school wolf submission to dominance.

I angle her face upward. "Look at me, babygirl. I want those pretty eyes on my face. I don't need you to show me deference." *You're my fucking mate.*

The moment our eyes lock a zing of electricity shoots through me. I scent her arousal again and barely keep in a groan. I should say goodnight, but I still hesitate. "Do you need anything?"

A long hard fuck?

My teeth in your shoulder?

Yeah, probably not.

"Just some sleep."

Right. Sleep.

I want to kiss her—badly—but I know she needs space. I settle for dropping a kiss on her forehead. "Goodnight, little wolf."

"Goodnight." She meets my gaze, but her glance is almost shy.

I wait until she shuts the door behind her before I force myself to move down the hall and into my bedroom.

It's going to be a long night.

COLLEEN

I find a toothbrush where Mark told me they would be and brush my teeth and wash my face, staring into the mirror some more, drinking in the changes in my appearance. I look younger. So much prettier. Almost normal. I find a comb and spend some time working it through my hair.

I hear the shower running in Mark's bathroom.

Back in the guest bedroom, my two pups are both already sound asleep. I kick off my shoes and walk around the bedroom, examining things. The room is basic, nothing personal on the dresser. Tasteful watercolor landscapes of Colorado scenes hang on the walls. They seem to all be by the same artist. I step closer to examine the signature on one. *Jeanne Ruhl.* His mother? Sister?

I want to go ask. I shouldn't miss being near a man I only just met, but I do.

Look at me, babygirl.

I love the way he talks to me—that deep voice so gravelly, heavy with sex and desire. He's a big male—stocky, with thick muscles that bulge under his uniform. I want to see him without the uniform, too. Which is a crazy thought, considering I've never taken an interest in a male. I was mated to Dirk far too young to ever want to think about males again.

I start to unbutton my jeans and pull them off, and then a foolish idea takes hold. Rebuttoning my jeans, I open the door and walk down the hall. The sound of the shower has stopped. "Mark?"

His door opens immediately. His short hair is wet, and he's wearing a soft blue t-shirt and a pair of boxers.

"What do you need, sweetheart?"

You. Being near him again both ignites and settles me. His coffee and leather scent permeates the room. I want more of what he gave to me on the chaise lounge. A glimpse into something carnal and beautiful that I've never felt before.

"Um, do you have a t-shirt I could sleep in?" It's not an excuse. I swear. It's not. I really just want to get out of these clothes, and I have nothing else to wear.

"Of course." He holds my gaze as he peels off the one he's wearing, causing my belly to do flip-flops. His chest appears even broader without the drape of fabric over it, and it bulges with muscles and is dusted with soft, dark curls. The urge to run my fingernails across them makes my fingers twitch.

I lick my lips, and his gaze tracks the movement, his eyes turning silver. I work to swallow as he holds the shirt out to me. "Thank you." I can't seem to make myself move to take it out of his hand. To walk back down the hall. All I can do is stare at the gorgeous man standing in front of me.

"Like what you see, babygirl?" His deep rumble

washes over me, making all my nerve endings tingle.

Afraid I will tumble forward, into his arms—into his bedroom—I snatch the t-shirt from his outstretched hand and swiftly walk back to my room. When I'm at the door, I stop and look over my shoulder, knowing he hasn't moved, sensing his gaze on my back. "Yes," I admit, before I open the door and slip inside, my heart pounding.

I detect a low rumble from him as he shuts his door. A growl, but not the menacing kind.

He wants me.

Dirk didn't want me. He used sex as another form of violence. It was a cruelty, never for either of our pleasure.

And I don't want to think about Dirk. I strip down to my panties and pull on Mark's large shirt, letting his scent wrap around me. I know he gave me this shirt on purpose. So I'd have his scent. He's trying to trigger my body's response. To show me he's my mate.

As if I didn't already know.

2

Mark

I wake late—which is totally unlike me, but I spent the entire night fucking my fist. Having my mate under my roof, sleeping in my guest bedroom, drove my wolf out of his mind. To make matters impossible, I knew my mate was touching herself, too. I scented her arousal and heard her quickened breath and restless movements through the door, and knowing she was probably as needy as I was drove me out of my mind.

I finally fell asleep as the sun was rising and got a few hours of shut-eye in.

Now, the smell of something sweet is coming from my kitchen. I yank on a pair of jeans and pad down the hall as I pull a shirt over my head. I detect the soft snore of her pups still coming from the guest bedroom.

I head down the stairs, and my dick goes horizontal—or as horizontal as possible trapped behind the denim—at what I find in the kitchen. Colleen is standing in a pair of panties and the oversized t-shirt I gave her to sleep in, flipping French toast in a frying pan. Last night when I locked myself in my bedroom to keep from barging in her room and helping her get satisfaction, I resolved to take things slow today. I don't know everything she's been through, but I can tell my mate has been terrorized for a long time.

She's not ready to trust, and she doesn't know me from Adam. Just because our biology tells us we're fated to be together doesn't mean she's willing or ready to accept that.

But seeing her like this—catching the earthy cinnamon notes of her delicious scent—aggression takes over. My need to pleasure her, mate her, mark her is all I can think of.

"Aw, babygirl," I rumble, stepping up against her back and filling one palm with the curve of her ass. I wrap my other arm around her waist to hold her captive against my chest. "I ought to spank this gorgeous ass for the cock-tease you're giving me right now." I massage her round cheeks, unable to stop the low rumbling growl in my chest. "You look so delectable this morning." My fingers trail below her cheeks to brush her most intimate parts.

The scent of her arousal perfumes the air, and

she throws her head back on my shoulder. She may not be emotionally ready for me, but her body already knows its master. I slide my hand down her panties in front to dip a finger in her wetness. "Would you like that, babygirl?" I murmur in her ear. "You need your wolf-daddy to pull these panties off you and spank your ass red?"

She moans softly.

"It would serve you right after the night I had. I barely slept with your scent wafting through my place like a drug."

Her juicy cunt squeezes around my finger. My cock presses against her back, dying to get in on the action. Fifty different ways to take my little she-wolf plow through my head—bent over the counter, up on the table with her legs spread wide, straddling my shoulders for a mustache ride. I'm so caught up in her little mewls of pleasure and the glorious feel of her slippery flesh beneath the pad of my finger that I fail to detect the sound of movement behind us.

"Leave her alone!" a small but fierce voice demands.

Colleen gasps. I release her and whirl to find Jayden standing at the foot of my stairs, his blue-green eyes wide and frightened, despite the angry slash of his brows. I draw in deep breaths to push back my lusty wolf, which probably shows in the color of my eyes.

"*Jayden,*" Colleen remonstrates. A blush turns her cheeks a pretty shade of pink, setting off her eyes, which are the same shade as her son's.

"It's okay." I wrap my hand around her nape and stroke my thumb along the column of her neck. To Jayden, I say, "She's all right. I wasn't hurting her. I would never hurt your momma."

"Apologize," Colleen instructs Jayden.

"No," I cut in, then backpedal. "I mean, I'm not trying to overrule your parenting, but I don't need an apology. He's protective of his momma— that's how it should be."

The boy looks uncertain but then must see something in his mother's face because the fear drops away. "Momma, your teeth!" he exclaims.

Colleen runs the tip of her tongue along her top teeth and smiles. "They grew in overnight."

My heart beats fiercely in my chest, the need to avenge the crimes against her warring with my satisfaction that her body has reset back to normal so quickly. One orgasm from her mate was all it took.

Just wait until I get my cum inside her. I try to push that filthy thought from my mind.

"Let me see," Angie cries, running down the stairs. She throws her arms around her mother's waist and looks up at Colleen's pretty smile.

I squeeze Colleen's nape before I release her. "I'm going to take another cold shower," I murmur.

At this point, I'm not sure a bucket of ice could cool me down. I leave Colleen to feed the pups and go back upstairs to get in my shower. Once there, I fist my cock, closing my eyes and leaning my forehead against the cool tile as cold water drenches my back. I beat off to the image of Colleen's legs, the ripeness of her sweet cunt, but something won't let me come. Which is a huge problem. There's no way I can be near her if I can't clear out some of this raging lust.

I groan, banging my head against the tile and fisting my cock even harder.

Her scent magically fills the shower as if conjured by my fantasies, mingling with the steam.

Mark. I hear my name spoken in her voice, the sound driving me wild.

No, wait. My eyes flare open, and I release my cock, spinning around.

She's standing in my bathroom, with the shirt off, wearing nothing but a pair of panties. I push the shower door open, but leave the water running to muffle the sounds I hope we're about to make. The kids have the keen hearing of shifters, but I hear them playing downstairs, and the shower noise will drown out our activity.

I step out, dripping wet. "Did you come for your spanking, little girl?"

Her nipples bead up, her long hair falls over one shoulder. "Yes."

I fucking love the new confidence she shows. Like she understands how much power she has over me. That she doesn't have to be afraid.

I want to go slowly—I *mean* to go slowly—but I'm too out of my mind with lust. I barrel into her, not taking time to dry off or be gentle. I grip her hips and spin her to face the counter. "Bend over, sweetheart," I tell her roughly.

By some miracle, she's still not afraid. She braces her hands on it and pushes her cute ass out. I stroke my hand over her panties. They're the practical kind—plain, cotton, heather grey.

"I'd better leave these on you, or we'll make too much noise," I tell her right before I lift my hand and crack it down on one side of her ass.

She makes an approving sound, *uhhnn*, and that's all I need to continue. I spank her hard and fast with one hand as my other dips down the front of her panties and rubs over her clit.

"Mark!" she gasps, her little button swelling under my fingertip, her pussy leaking the most delicious juices.

"Say it again," I command, spanking harder. "Who's your daddy?"

She presses her fingers over the top of mine with a desperate whine. "You are. Mark. You're my daddy."

Oh, fates, I'm going to lose it. I'm going to lose control and sink my teeth in her. But the moment my gaze goes to her shoulder and tracks the scars her asshole ex left, I regain control.

Her teeth grew in, but those scars still haven't healed, which means they run deep. I'm going to take that asshole alpha ex-mate of hers out for what he's done to Colleen and his pups.

And I won't betray her trust. Ever.

I channel my need into spanking her harder and faster, knowing a she-wolf *loves* a little pain with her pleasure, remembering how her pussy turned molten when I threatened it downstairs.

I sink two fingers inside her with my other hand, cupping her mons and pressing over her swollen clit.

"Please," she pleads, and I stop spanking, in case she's begging for mercy. "No," she says quickly. "Don't stop. I need it—please."

"What do you need, babygirl?" I thrust my fingers deeper inside her as I squeeze and knead her ass.

She twists to look over her shoulder, and her gaze drops to my erection.

"You want a long, wet ride on my cock, babygirl?"

She licks her lips, making me groan. "Yes, please."

Yes, please. This girl.

I yank a drawer open to find a box of condoms and roll one on as my beautiful she-wolf shimmies out of her panties. Fates, I hope I can control myself.

But Colleen trusts me, and that makes me desperate to be worthy of that faith. I know it can't be easy for her. I drag the head of my sheathed cock through her juices. "Is this what you need, sweetheart? Daddy's cock?"

"Yes, please."

I push her lower back to angle her ass up more, then shove in, filling her. I have to stop, closing my eyes and willing back the need to mark her. My teeth are long and extended in my mouth, dripping with the serum that contains my scent, that would forever mark her as mine.

"Please," she begs.

Fuck.

I wrap my arm around the front of her hips to keep them from slamming against the hard counter, and then I drill into her like our lives depend on it. Maybe they do. I find one of her nipples with my free hand and squeeze and pinch it. "Baby," I rasp. Being inside her is doing crazy things to me.

Nothing has ever felt so right. The need to satisfy her, to satisfy myself overwhelms me.

"Yes!" she whisper-shouts, eyes closed. The sight of her expression in the mirror as she's about to orgasm sends me over the edge.

I hold in my roar as I fuck her hard and fast, shifting my hand between her legs to rub her clit.

Her mouth opens in a silent "O," and her muscles start squeezing around my dick. I slam in hard and stay, rubbing her clit and watching in the mirror as we both hurtle over the edge into ecstasy.

I throw my head back, but it rebounds and time blurs as I realize I'm about to mark my female. I manage to cover her shoulder with my palm right before I strike, driving my fangs into the back of my hand.

"Oh!" Colleen's cry of dismay makes me pull out and step back.

She whirls, her nostrils flaring at the scent of my blood. Her eyes widen when she catches sight of my self-inflicted wounds. "Mark."

"I'm sorry, baby. It happened so fast, I thought I had it under control."

She grabs my hand and examines it, her brows knit. "You bit... *yourself*."

"Well, yeah. I wasn't going to bite you. Not without your permission."

She's gone stiff now. Tension shows in the set of her shoulders. "You can't mark me. Not now, not ever."

COLLEEN

Mark shows nothing outwardly, but I sense his pain like a sharp knife to the gut. I expect him to walk away. Or try to hurt me. Or do any of the normal things people do when you push them away, but instead he picks me up by the waist and sits me on the bathroom counter.

"Why not, babygirl?" He cages me between his arms, leaning his hands on the quartz.

I try to swallow around the lump in my throat. "I don't want that." I curse the quaver in my voice.

He cups both sides of my face, cradling it so gently I want to weep. Lowering his head to mine, he murmurs, "You know I'm your mate."

Tears pop into my eyes. "I don't know anything." My lips tremble, inches from his.

"You're lying." It's no more than a whisper. He's trying to coax honesty out of me, but I just can't give it. It's not safe. Not for him, not for me, not for my pups.

I turn my face away, but he gently turns it back.

No one has ever held me so tenderly. Touched me with such reverence. The sex was incredible, but this? It guts me.

"Let me take care of you, babygirl."

Babygirl. He called himself Daddy earlier after he spanked me. I don't know anything about this dynamic, but both my body and my being respond like I've just found home.

Tears spill from my eyes. I'm crying because I can't accept his offer, no matter how badly I want to. Not until I somehow get free from Dirk.

He thumbs away my tears. "Please."

I duck my head and revert to what I know—showing deference to the alpha. "May I take a shower now?"

I sense his frown before I peek at it. He studies me for a moment, the corners of his mouth downturned. This is where I'm sure he'll walk away, but he still doesn't. He scoops me from the counter and carries me into the shower where he lowers me gently to my feet and begins to soap every inch of my body.

I whimper at the sweetness of it. The delicious caress. Having my mate naked in a small space with me. My legs tremble as he slides his hands up my inner thighs, stroking softly when he reaches the apex. He kisses between my legs, but doesn't bring me to orgasm like he did at the pool last night. Instead, he continues the slow torture of worshipping my body.

"We don't know each other, babygirl. But I know you're mine. And I'm sure you know it, too. Let me in, sweetheart."

"Please," I weep. Because he's killing me. Because I want to say *yes* so badly. I want to be his, to let him mark me, take care of me, call me babygirl and treat me with both passion and tenderness.

He stands and wraps his arms around me, sliding his fingers into the cleft of my ass, soaping my most intimate place. "I don't believe you," he says. When I search his gaze to understand what he doesn't believe, he says, "I don't believe you want me to stand down. But I will, babygirl. Because I need you to feel safe. I need you to know I'll honor your wishes." The entire time he speaks, he runs his fingers over my anus, sudsing between my cheeks.

I whimper. My bare breasts press against his muscled torso. I drag my lips over the soft hair of his chest.

He curves his fingers lower and sweeps them between my legs. "I'm keeping a tally of your lies, little girl." His fingers brush over my opening. I press closer to him, hoping he'll take me again. "There will be a reckoning."

The way he says it makes punishment sound more like some delicious reward. Of course, I just learned what it feels like to be spanked by him, and I adored it.

I lift my face, letting water stream over it. "What kind of reckoning?" I hardly recognize my own voice, it sounds so husky.

He moves his finger back up to my asshole and circles there. "The kind that ends with this gorgeous ass red and hot and my cock buried deep between these cheeks."

I almost orgasm right there. Just from his threatened punishment, which sounds far more like a reward than anything. I reach down to take care of my own needs, since he seems more inclined to tease, but he catches my wrist. "Uh uh. Not when you've been naughty, little wolf. No more pleasure for you until I decide you can come."

A mini-orgasm rips through me, and I shiver against him, catching my breath.

Mark chuckles darkly. "That goes on your ledger, babygirl. Disobedience."

He releases me and positions me away from the spray of water to shampoo my hair. I close my eyes, too dazed with lust and confusion to do anything else. When he's finished, he turns off the water and wraps me in a warm, fuzzy towel.

"We'll go to Target to buy clothes and necessities for the three of you today," he tells me.

I nod, not trusting myself to speak.

"And then, I'd like to take the pups to do something fun. Would they like an amusement park? Or mini-golf?"

I stare at him. Both options seem outlandish to me. So outlandish, I almost giggle. This is no time for an amusement park. I have to keep my children hidden from their psychopathic father. And yet, the idea of denying my kids such an extravagance feels cruel. Our life in Kentucky with Dirk was horrible, but moving away and staying on the run hasn't been a picnic, either. My sister gave me enough money to get away, but because Dirk's an alpha, I was afraid to ask other shifters for assistance.

Cody, the alpha in Colorado Springs, found us

by accident and gave me money and his help, but until then, we were struggling just to eat.

Maybe we could go have some fun. Just this once. I know we can't stay here with Mark—not permanently. This is just a temporary resting place while I wait to see if Dirk knows where I am and if he's coming for us. We may have to run again. Maybe soon.

"That would be nice," I tell him.

He lowers his head and brushes his lips across mine. It's another tease because I don't get a real kiss. He tucks the towel around me, turns me around and smacks my ass to send me out the door of his bathroom.

I send a small smile over my shoulder as I scoot back to the guest bathroom where I left yesterday's clothes. I put them on and open the door to the guest bedroom.

Jayden and Angie are playing Kings on the Corners card game on the bed. "Go and jump in the shower," I tell Jayden. "Mark is going to take us shopping and then to do something fun."

"What?" Angie demands as Jayden scrambles off the bed.

"It's a surprise. I'll let him tell you," I say. "You'll like it."

"What is it? What is it?" Angie starts bouncing up and down on the bed as I pull my clothes on.

"Don't!" I say automatically, that familiar rush

of adrenaline kicking in, my frayed nerves firing in protective fear. "Don't jump on the bed, angel."

"She can jump." Mark leans in the doorway, dressed in a black t-shirt that molds to his muscles and a faded pair of jeans. He looks sinfully handsome, but more than that, his indulgent smile as he watches Angie makes my eyes smart again.

It's too late, though. Angie heard the fear in my voice and came down off the bed to glue herself to my side. "What's the surprise?" she whispers to me.

Mark winks. "I'll wait until your brother is out of the shower, and then you two can vote."

"There's only two of us," Angie says, warming to Mark far more quickly than I would expect. "Who's the tie-breaker?"

"Your mom," Mark says immediately, pushing off the door frame and sauntering down the stairs.

My need to follow him, to stay close to the warm sphere of energy he projects makes me rock on my feet. But I need to call my sister—to find out if she's heard anything about us through my dad's pack.

I take my burner phone into Mark's backyard to call Meagan. He watches me through the window, like he's afraid to take his eyes off me, but it doesn't feel controlling. Just protective.

I let Angie come out with me, and she starts picking up fallen leaves, examining them and comparing their colors.

"Hello?" It's a new number, so my sister doesn't recognize it.

"Can you talk?"

"Hang on a sec." I hear the bang of a door, and my sister's footsteps crunching over leaves. I picture her walking out the back door of the little cabin she shares with her mate and two small pups toward the woods. "Okay, I'm good. How's it going?"

"Have you heard anything? About me, I mean?"

Meagan is still part of our father's pack, the second largest pack in Kentucky. She stayed at home and mated her high school boyfriend after getting pregnant. They're not fated mates, but they do love each other and make a good match.

The largest pack in Kentucky belongs to Dirk, which is why my father offered me up to be mated to him in some kind of medieval uniting of kingdoms. Things were horrible right from the start, but I couldn't tell my father because Dirk told me he'd kill my father and take over his pack if he ever challenged him.

"No, is everything okay?"

I breathe a sigh of relief. "Good. Yes. Well, no. Jayden got hit by a car and was taken to a hospital —he's fine, of course—but I was afraid word might somehow get back to Dirk if he'd filed a missing persons report."

Meagan scoffs. "He wouldn't do that. He told

Dad that you two had a misunderstanding, and you were being stubborn, but you'd be home soon." Meagan hesitates a moment then adds "I know you didn't want me to, but I finally told Dad the truth. I told him what Dirk had done to you and that you three were running for your lives. Dad's beside himself. He hasn't gone over to challenge Dirk yet because he needs proof to show the pack if there's going to be a war."

I swear softly. "I don't want a pack war over me, Meagan. Dad's pack won't win. Dirk would kill Dad just to hurt me."

Meagan's quiet. "I know. But Dad has the right to know. And now that you're out of that house, I feel like it's time to stop keeping the horrible secret."

Tears spear my eyes. "Don't let him challenge Dirk," I beg. "Promise me."

"I'll do what I can. What about the humans at the hospital? Did anyone witness Jayden's healing?"

"No. I called the alpha in Colorado Springs, and he just came and pulled us out of there before Jayden got checked or anything."

"That's a close call. So you're under his protection?"

"Not exactly." I glance toward the house, everything warming as I think about Mark. "I'm in Denver… with my mate."

Meagan gasps. "Oh my God. Are you serious?"

Her excitement practically vibrates through the phone.

"Yeah, but Meagan, what am I going to do? Dirk will kill us both if I let him mark me."

Meagan goes quiet for a moment then says fiercely, "Fuck Dirk. Why did you leave him if you're not going to live? Are you just going to stay in hiding for the rest of your life?"

"I'm just trying to keep my pups safe and alive!" I cry, angry tears forcing their way to the outer corners of my eyes.

"Fuck. I know. I'm sorry. I'm so sorry," Meagan soothes, even though I'm the older sister. She's the only reason I was able to get away. She brought me enough cash to get bus tickets to Colorado and to pay the first month's rent on an apartment. We didn't have time to plan things out—it was a hasty decision after Dirk got violent with me and Jayden.

"I gotta go. Let me know if you hear anything."

"This is your new phone?"

"Yes."

"What's his name? Your mate, I mean."

"Mark. Mark Ruhl. He's a DEA agent and a shifter council enforcer. He's older. Like in his forties."

"A silver wolf."

I can't stop the way my lips curve thinking of him. The way I'm instantly soothed from the anxiety of a moment before. "Not too much silver, but yeah. Super hot silver wolf. And he likes to be called *Daddy*."

"Oh my gawd. That's so hot."

"Super hot." I laugh. It's the first time I've ever had anything sexual or fun to share with Meagan. I was just out of high school when my dad pawned me off, and I couldn't share the joy of Meagan's exploits when she started sleeping with her mate because my life was so traumatic by then.

"Let him mark you, Co-co. You can't delay living forever. At some point, you have to claim your own life."

I don't answer because my sister can't even begin to understand the mental slavery I've been in for so long now, and I'm not going to defend myself.

"Love you," I say simply.

"I love you, too. Text me a pic of Mark. I promise I'll delete it as soon as it comes through."

I laugh softly because it's the best thing I've ever had to text my sister about. "I will. Bye."

3

Mark

The four of us stand in line for the Dragon Wing, one of the rides at Elitch Gardens, Denver's amusement park. The pups are on a high from waffle cones filled with ice cream and the five rides we've already been on.

Colleen's face goes soft and beautiful every time she looks at them.

"You look younger, Momma," Angie tells her, looking up. She's as cute as they come, with a blonde ponytail high on her head and the same big blue-green eyes as her mom and brother. I'm already as fiercely protective of the pups as I am of my unclaimed mate.

I rest a hand lightly on her hip. She does look younger. Every hour seems to roll back the effects of time on her appearance. "How old are you, babygirl?"

"Twenty-eight."

I glance at the boy. "How old are you, Jayden?"

"Nine and a half."

The rattle of the ride keeps the humans around us from hearing the growl in my throat. The wolves hear it though, and all three of them stare at me.

"I was eighteen when my father arranged my mating," Colleen says, correctly guessing at the cause of my rage. "Just legal."

"Was that… normal in your pack?" I ask through clenched teeth. I want to kill both her father and the alpha who claimed her.

She shakes her head. "I don't know. It was horrible for me. I had to forget about college and leave everyone I knew to live with a tyrant."

The kids listen with big eyes, like they've never heard this before.

"You mean Dad?" Jayden asks softly.

She nods. "He had just become alpha of his pack after his father was killed. He was worried about his position being challenged because he was young to lead a pack. He went to grandpa, and they made some kind of deal."

"We're not going back there, right, Momma?" Angie asks.

"Never," she promises, and one small part of me relaxes. At least we agree on that.

"You're going to stay with me now," I say firmly, even though Colleen hasn't accepted it yet.

Jayden stays silent, but he watches me with that wary gaze.

"Are we, Momma?" Angie asks.

Colleen looks away, her lips pressing together. "We'll see," she murmurs.

"Can we keep the bikes?" Angie wants to know.

I bought both the kids bikes this morning at Target. I put everything any one of them looked at or picked up in the cart. Colleen took about half the things back out, but when I picked up the two bikes, she didn't dare override me. Not when her kids looked so excited.

She just stood there with tear-bright eyes and nibbled on her lips.

"The bikes are yours," I say. "No matter what. But I want you to stay." It's our turn at the front of the line. I escort the pups forward then hold Colleen back. "We'll wait for you where it gets out," I tell Jayden. "Take care of your sister."

He nods, like the responsibility was his honor. He's an amazing kid.

I put my arm around Colleen and usher her to the place where the ride lets out. "For every lie, you owe me a truth," I tell her.

"I didn't li—"

I stop her with a finger on her lips. "Don't do it again. Remember my tally."

Her lips move up at the corners, but her smile is sad. I would bust this world apart to figure out how to make it shine.

She turns into me and puts her hands on my chest. "A truth," she murmurs. "Okay. Here's a truth. I never orgasmed with a male before last night. You were my first."

Aw, fuck. I shouldn't be so goddamn proud—it's been over twenty years since I first learned how to get a female off—but I am.

I wrap my arms around her and hold her against my body. Her cinnamon scent nearly turns me feral. "That's a good one, babygirl." But because I'm a greedy fucker, I push for more. "Give me another one. Tell me something, angel. Are you not sure of me or not sure what you want?"

Pain flits across her face, and the need to avenge her for every wrong ever inflicted nearly makes my wolf canines pop out. "Not sure of what I want," she croaks in a rusty voice, but it smells like a lie.

I narrow my eyes, thinking hard. She doesn't seem scared of me, so it must be something else. I have to prove myself in some other way.

If only I could get her to open up, to tell me what's going on in that gorgeous head of hers.

"One more," I say.

Vulnerability flashes in her eyes, like I'm asking far too much of her. "What is it?"

"If your future hadn't been sold at age eighteen, what would you have done with it?"

Her lips tremble, and she rolls them inward to hide it. "I don't know. I planned to go to college, but I hadn't figured out what I wanted to study. I wanted to get out of our small town, maybe live in the human world. Earn a decent living."

"What did you like in school?"

She shrugs. "I was good at math and science. I liked to draw. I thought maybe I could go into architecture or engineering. But that ship has sailed."

The gate opens, and people pour off the ride. She pulls away from me to open her arms for Angie, who barrels into them.

"Right. Ride over. Okay. What's next, kids?" I ask, letting them lead.

I didn't think I'd have pups or a mate. At age forty, I'd long since discarded any hope of a family, but here I'd found my mate, and she came with two precious pups. I'd thought my calling was law enforcement, but that all changed yesterday.

Now I'm sure of my life's purpose. It's these three shifters right here. I just have to get them to let me care for them.

At the next ride, I excuse myself to make a call.

"Jenson, it's Mark Ruhl." Jenson is on the shifter council. He's an old bear shifter from Wyoming and is the councilmember who I report to.

"What's up?"

"There's a she-wolf and two pups under my protection. They ran away from an abusive male—the alpha of a pack outside of Lexington, Kentucky."

"The council doesn't get involved in domestic quarrels."

"I'm not asking the council to get involved. I'm putting the council on notice. I will not hesitate to put that alpha down if he comes near her again."

Jenson is silent for a long moment, then he blows out his breath. "Noted."

"That's it," I say and end the call.

Due process doesn't exist in the shifter world. Generally problems are solved by physical aggression. But seventy years ago, when the human population began to grow and spread and bleed into shifter territories, the council was formed. It's less about governing our own than it is about keeping shifters out of trouble with humans. I'm the guy who puts down shifters who go feral. Or who murder or take advantage of humans. I might not have owed the council an explanation for defending my mate, but putting them on notice in advance may help with any fallout.

Still, I hope it doesn't come to that. I don't want Jayden and Angie to have to live with the male who killed their father. That doesn't sit well with me.

But neither does having that man looming over Colleen and the pups as a constant fear. The sooner this gets solved, the better.

COLLEEN

The pups are exhausted by the time I get them to bed. The amusement park and a steak dinner at Outback wore them out.

Mark caught me before I followed them up the stairs to the guest room. He wrapped a fist in my hair and tugged my head backward. "I'm going to need you in my bed tonight, babygirl—don't even think of refusing me," he growled, turning my insides to molten lava. Then he trailed his tongue over my pulse. "After the pups are asleep. In my room. Understand?" He slid his fingers between my legs and pushed the seam of my jeans against my clit.

"Y-yes," I answered.

Now, as I push the door to his bedroom open without knocking, my heart pounds against my chest.

Mark's demand sounded lustful, not angry. His brand of dominance never scares me. Never offends me. It just makes my nipples hard and my panties damp.

So even though I know walking into his bedroom at night is a bad idea considering every time I get near him I risk being marked—I do it anyway.

"Clothes off." Mark speaks from the doorway to the bathroom. He's taken another shower. Either he has obsessive compulsive tendencies toward cleanliness, or he really is using cold showers to tamp down his lust. I prefer to believe it's the latter although I don't mind the clean part. The scent of soap that mingles with his deliciously male aroma.

I unbutton the new skinny jeans he bought me and shimmy out of them. I'm wearing a pair of red satin panties and a matching bra—also his purchase—and when he sees me in them, his eyes turn silver.

"What color is your wolf?" I ask.

"Black. Yours?"

"Tan."

He stalks closer. "I haven't seen your wolf eyes yet."

No. I still don't know if I can shift. I haven't shifted in years. Another byproduct of being mated to Dirk. It's the reason my healing fled. But maybe now... maybe my true fated mate has already healed me.

I stand in my new bra and panties, my knees trembling for him.

He shakes his head and spins me to face the bed, pushing my torso down. "I didn't say you could leave the panties on tonight." His hand crashes down on my ass, sharp and punitive.

A little sound of protest leaves my lips, but Mark has forgotten to be careful with me. His wolf is going feral, and it's running the show. His dominance doesn't produce even an ounce of fear in me, though. It feels natural. His wolf comes to the surface because he wants me so badly, not because he needs to hurt me. I somehow know if I protested, he'd pull back immediately.

He slaps me again on the other cheek, even harder. "Did I, babygirl?"

"No, Daddy." The moniker just rolls off my tongue, but it feels right. I like calling Mark *Daddy*. I like the idea of Mark being my daddy. Protective. Caring. Dirty and demanding when it comes to sex. Fates, it's only been twenty-four hours, but this male has already wormed his way into my very guarded heart. And it's not just the pheromones talking.

Mark growls his approval, yanking my panties down my legs. "Aw, damn, babygirl. You're going to get yourself fucked so hard you won't be able to walk straight." He peppers my ass with hard spanks, and each one lights another match of lust within me, the flames threatening to engulf me. My vision sharpens and domes, and I know my eyes have changed color, too.

My she-wolf is back.

She wants to be claimed.

"Panties *off*," Mark chokes, frustration and lust thickening his voice.

I scramble to get my panties from my thighs to my ankles, and the moment I do, he kicks my feet wider.

I smother a shriek when he spanks my pussy, the wetness making a sticky sound.

"When I tell you clothes off, I need you bare, baby. How else am I going to lick this pussy until you scream?" He hooks his thumbs inside my cheeks and spreads me wide, making me arch and expose my sex.

And then his mouth is on me, his neatly trimmed beard scratching my sensitive skin as his tongue sweeps between my legs. He kneads and roughly squeezes my ass, all the while flicking his tongue over my clit, sucking my labia, nipping me. Every now and then, he delivers another stinging slap to my ass or thigh, mingling pain with pleasure. Danger with excitement.

Only the danger isn't that he'll harm me. It's that he'll claim me.

But it's too late for me to stop things or even slow them down. I'm half-crazed for him now, too, moaning and needy, ready to beg for what he wanted to deny me of this morning.

"*Colleen.*" Mark sounds desperate. His wolf may start to go mad if I keep denying him what it craves. I think he's going to ask for my consent, to mark me with his teeth, but instead he says, "I need to come inside you this time. Will you let me do that?"

At first my sex-scrambled brain doesn't even understand the question, but then it dawns on me— he wore a condom last night.

"Yes," I say, consequences be damned. I need to feel all of him, no barrier between us.

I hear the soft rustle of fabric, and then he shoves inside me. I buck against him, loving the sensation of being filled. Nothing has ever felt so right in my life, but then he pulls out again.

"I need to see your face, babygirl." He flips me around, propping my ass on the edge of the bed before he shoves in again. I rest back on my elbows, watching the place our bodies connect. His thickness. The way my petals part and stretch to accept him. The scent of my arousal.

Mark's silver gaze sweeps up my body, and then he frowns. "*Why are you wearing that bra?*"

I can't help it. I giggle. Because Mark's pseudo-anger of the state of my undress makes me feel coveted and gorgeous. "I thought you liked this bra." I pull the cups of my bra down to show him my peaked nipples. "Your eyes turned silver when I picked it out."

"Take it off, or I tear it off," he threatens. "I like it too goddamn much."

I unsnap it and slide my arms out, tossing it to the side. "Yes, Daddy."

His grip on my upper thighs turns brutal, but I'm not afraid. I sense the passion behind it, not anger or violence. He slams in hard and fast. "Play with them," he growls. It takes me a second to understand, and then I moan as I obey, weighing my breasts, squeezing them, pinching my own nipples.

"I'm going to come inside you. I need to mark you in some way, and you're damn well going to take it."

I'm thrilled by his demand because his respect for my wishes is still so clearly there. He won't mark me, even though it's killing him. I also suspect he's warning me in case I choose to object.

And I should. But no part of me wants to. Fate sent me this mate, and I'm willing to roll the dice to see if Fate wants to give me a pup with him. Being a mother is the only thing I've loved about the last ten years.

I reach down and make a V with my fingers around the place where his cock enters me, wanting to feel him with all of me.

He roars, his movements growing jerky. "Fuck, little wolf. You're driving me crazy." He rubs his thumb over my clit and I orgasm, my muscles squeezing around his dick. He comes at the same time, and I swear to Fate I feel every hot drop of cum that shoots inside me. It sears me. Sizzles and pops and changes me. So much heat floods through me that my vision turns black with fireworks exploding around the edges. And then pleasure. Oceans of it, washing over me, cleaning me, clearing me, leaving only the purity of my essence and his. Fated mates.

Something makes me touch my shoulder, the place where the skin was knotted with scar tissue from repeated dry bites. Only a true fated mate will cause a male wolf to produce the serum that leaves his scent in his female's flesh. Dirk wasn't my fated mate, but that didn't stop him from savaging my shoulder every time he forced himself on me. After a few years, I just stopped healing. But now my shoulder is as smooth as a baby's skin. Soft, supple. Reborn.

Mark's panting, eyes still silver, his canines long. "When I mark you, babygirl, it won't be there."

I blink up at him. "No?"

"No." He shakes his head. "I'll mark this cute little ass." He slides his hands under my butt and squeezes both cheeks in his large hands.

"Oh." I start to laugh, then. Almost hysterically. It's relief and joy and nerves bundled into one. "You're an ass man," I say.

The brown of Mark's eyes return, and he grins at me. "You could say that." He eases out. "I want you in my bed tonight," he says, somehow correctly guessing that I plan to make a run for it back to the guest room. "I won't mark you. You can trust me. But I need you here."

I think about my pups. But they're deep asleep, exhausted by the fun of the day. They don't need me.

And the thought of sleeping beside Mark makes my she-wolf...

I spontaneously shift just thinking about her.

It's the first time in years, and my wolf is so happy, she turns in circles on the bed before flopping to her side and offering her belly up.

"Hey beautiful," Mark croons, stroking my face and belly, rubbing my ears. "You're so gorgeous. I can't wait to run and hunt with you."

I will myself to shift back, and it happens with ease. As if I'd never lost my wolf, never lost the ability to shift at will. To heal. To be who I truly am.

"Oh Fates." I sit up and cover my face with my hands, happy tears running down my cheeks.

Mark's smile fades, and he crawls on the bed with me, prying my hands from my face. "Fuck, baby. Had you lost your wolf? Is that why you couldn't heal?"

I nod through the tears. "It's been four years."

He kisses them away and pulls me into his arms. "Never again, angel. You'll never lose her again. She was always with you."

"You brought her back out," I say.

"*We* did," he says. "I can't believe I found you. I feel so blessed."

I want to feel blessed too, but there's still a shadow looming over me. Over us. And that's the part I hate. I care far too much about Mark to let him risk his life for us.

4

Mark

I may have promised not to mark my sweet mate, but that didn't stop me from fucking her twice more by morning.

She curls into me, nuzzling my neck. "What made you enter law enforcement?" she asks. "And which came first, being enforcer, or working for the DEA?"

I burrow my fingers in her hair and massage the back of her head. "DEA came first then enforcer. The council loved the idea of having me in human law enforcement as a means of helping to hide shifter activities when they go outside human law."

"And how did you end up with the DEA?" she asks.

"I grew up near here, in a western suburb of Denver that bordered the foothills, so we could run

57

and hunt. Our high school was mixed—human and shifter—and my best friend was a human."

Colleen lifts her lovely face, her blue-green eyes trained on mine. She braces, like she already knows what I'm going to say.

"We were just screwing around, partying. Of course, drugs had no effect on me, but I figured my job was to keep them safe. Be designated driver. The guy who kept a clear head. My friends didn't know I was a shifter. Our recreational use had sort of escalated from pot to sampling a little cocaine. I guess it had been laced with something else. It burned my nose, and I felt sick for a few minutes. But my buddy…"

Colleen holds her breath.

I nod my confirmation. "He died. And that's when I vowed to take down drug traffickers." I shrug. "I guess I blamed them for what happened."

She lays her cheek against my bare chest. "What was his name?"

"Travis."

"I'm sorry for your loss."

I massage her scalp some more. "It was a long time ago."

"You're noble—working for the greater good." She trails a fingertip through the hair on my chest.

"Your greater good is all I care about now," I tell her.

"You take care of the people you love—even humans. Is that why you call yourself, Daddy?"

I shrug. "I guess. I'm alpha, so I like to be in charge, but in a way that's caretaking and kind. I want to spoil you."

"That sounds wonderful." Her smile is sad, which sends my wolf into a panic.

"I can call into work today," I tell her. I don't want to leave her and the kids alone. Unprotected. And the truth is, I'm half-afraid she'll be gone by the time I get back.

She shakes her head. "No. You were going to check on our records. To make sure Dirk hasn't filed a missing person report."

I nod and scrub a hand over my face. "Yes. I will. If he has, we'll file a restraining order. Is he the type to go by human laws?"

"No," she admits. "He probably never filed anything. My sister says he told our father we had a disagreement, and I'll be back. He's downplaying the whole thing. But you never know. He could change his story at any moment. He's a psychopath."

"I'm going to take care of him," I say grimly.

"No," she says quickly and prickles of cold race over my skin.

I stare at her, trying to work things out in my head, but I don't have enough fucking information to go on. I pick up her hand and kiss the back of it. "Talk to me, Colleen."

A world of regret swims in her eyes, and my stomach tightens like a fist.

When she doesn't answer, I ask, "Do you love him?"

The horror on her face as she scoffs soothes some of my agitation.

"I don't have to kill him," I say. "There are other ways to handle this." There probably aren't, but if she wants to keep the father of her pups alive for their sake, I understand. I won't fight her on it. I'll figure something out, so she feels safe, and he lives.

I go to my gun safe and unlock it to retrieve my gun for work. Sensing Colleen behind me, I turn. She's staring into the safe.

"Is that the pistol?" she asks. When I just stare at her, she says, "the one with silver bullets?" Silver bullets are forbidden, except to enforcers.

I scrub my face, a tingling of foreboding going through me at her interest. "Yeah, babygirl. That's the pistol." I study her face, but she turns away, nodding.

"Call or text me if you need anything. We'll work on getting you your own car this week, okay?"

I can't stand this itchy feeling I have that Colleen sees staying at my place as a temporary stop. A place to crash until she figures out her next move. I don't know what it will take to change her mind about that—about me—but I'm trying to make the idea of staying as appealing as possible.

She nods but wears that same wary look her son often gives me. Like she's waiting for some inevitable disaster.

Of course, she's right. Trouble is coming. But I welcome it. Because the sooner it comes, the sooner I can quash it and show Colleen I'm prepared to do whatever it takes to keep her safe and happy.

∼

COLLEEN

Mark's house feels empty without him, but the kids are anxious to try out the new bikes, so I get outside and enjoy the autumn air as they ride around the neighborhood.

When I get back to the house, I find my sister has called. Seven times.

Fuck.

I hit the call button and pace around Mark's kitchen.

"He knows where you are." Meagan foregoes any greeting to deliver the news that hits me like a punch to the gut.

"From the hospital?"

"No, I don't think so. Dirk told Dad that he had word you'd been kidnapped by the Denver pack and were being held against your will. I guess he heard it from someone on the shifter council or something. Colleen, he's already on a flight over there, and he's got everyone in his pack driving through the night to meet him there."

Despair rolls through me. "No."

"He wanted Dad to get his pack to drive over as well, but Dad cussed him out and got himself on a plane, too."

My mind races. "Okay, thanks for the information."

"What are you going to do?" Meagan's voice takes on a note of panic, like she's already guessing at my plans.

"All I know is that I'm not going to let this turn into a war between packs. The Denver pack doesn't know me at all, and it's not fair to ask them to fight for me. I don't even know for sure that they would."

"For once, you need to stop worrying about wars between packs. The reason we have packs is to protect our members. I think you should accept the help that's being offered to you. Especially if the Denver pack is big enough."

"I'm not comfortable with that. I'll keep you posted." I hang up before she can argue more.

My stomach roils as a dark wave of grief crashes over me.

Leaving Mark is going to tear my she-wolf in two. But I won't have him risk his life to protect us.

Not when Dirk's bringing his whole pack. Even with silver bullets, it's not a war he can win alone.

I go to Mark's bedroom. I memorized the code for the safe this morning when he opened it, so I use it now to get in, carefully taking out the pistol and silver bullets. My best bet is to take care of this situation on my own. And I now have the means to do it.

I load the gun and tuck it in my waistband, then head downstairs to write a note for Mark and talk to the kids.

"Angie, Jayden, come here, please." After I write the note, I summon the pups from where they were watching television and sit down on a kitchen chair.

They must hear something different in my voice because all the joy of the bike ride instantly disappears. Jayden turns off the TV, and they both come to stand in front of me. I gather them close to me.

"Are we leaving?" Jayden asks quietly.

"I need to take care of something. Something really important. It's not safe for you two to come along."

Angie's eyes fill with tears.

Jayden's expression makes him look ancient. "Is Dad here?"

I swallow then nod. "I'm going to deal with him."

"With Mark's gun?" Jayden asks, surprising me.

He must've heard Mark and I talking about it in the hallway Saturday night.

I nod again.

"What if it doesn't work?"

"*It has to work*," I say fiercely. Because there's no other option. I don't want to keep running and hiding for the rest of our lives. I met my true mate, my fated mate, my wolf-daddy, and I need to be with him.

"I'm leaving this note for Mark. When he gets home, give it to him, okay?"

Jayden nods gravely.

Angie's crying for real now.

I refuse to let my own tears fall. There's no way I'm taking them with me because if I fail, they'd be in Dirk's hands. This way, if something goes wrong, Mark will protect them and call my sister, who will take them. But no, nothing can go wrong. I'll be back for them. They need me. I hug them both tightly and kiss the tops of their heads, and then I schedule a ride on my ride sharing app for the mountains. I need to get away from humans to make this work.

5

Mark

I get a bad feeling in the afternoon, one that compounds when Colleen doesn't answer her phone. I end up leaving work early, claiming I have a doctor's appointment, and drive straight home.

My mate wouldn't leave. She couldn't. Our wolves need each other, and she wouldn't be safe on her own.

That's what I tell myself the whole ride home, but cold dread fills my limbs. I park in the garage and throw the door open, relief coursing through me when I hear the television and see the kids.

But then I instantly recognize something's wrong. Both pups look frightened. I sniff the air, but there's no scent of another wolf. Colleen's scent is faint.

"Where's your mom?" I try to keep my voice even despite my returning panic.

Jayden stands and walks to the kitchen table, rather than answer me. He picks up a sealed envelope with my name on it.

Fuck.

I snatch it from his fingers, jogging upstairs to my bedroom, already knowing what I'll find. The safe is open; the gun, gone.

I tear the envelope open and read Colleen's neat writing.

Mark,

Dirk's pack is on the way from Kentucky. Please do not engage with them. I don't want a pack war. I will take care of him myself.

If for some reason I don't make it back, my sister Meagan's number is below. She will arrange for the pups. I'm sorry to leave them with you, but I can't let Dirk take them.

Thank you for everything,

Colleen

Thank you for everything? What the fuck? I hate the formal sound of the letter, like I am some stranger, not her goddamn mate. But that isn't the part that has me frantic.

It's knowing what my brave, beautiful mate is trying to do. *Fuck!*

I need to get to her. Stop her.

I put a tracker in her phone the morning after she arrived, fearing something like this would happen. I rush to open the app and draw a sharp breath when I see where she's gone. She headed toward the mountains, about twenty miles west of Denver.

"Jayden, Angie, I'm going after your mother. I'll bring her home safely. I'm going to call someone from my pack to come over and stay with you. Answer my call if this rings, understand?" I hand Jayden a tablet that I can call him on. "You can download games and play on that, if you want, or just keep watching TV."

Jayden nods. Angie just watches me with big eyes. "I'm scared," she says.

"Oh baby." I kneel down in front of her and draw her into a hug. "I'm going to make sure you're safe."

"What about Momma?"

"I'm going to get her now." I kiss the top of her head. "We'll be back."

I wish I felt half as sure as I sound. I run out to my SUV and jump in, starting it and backing up before I even have my seat belt on. As I drive, I punch in the number for Meagan that Colleen left me.

"Hello?" The female voice that answers sounds alarmed.

"Meagan? This is Mark Ruhl, I'm—"

"Colleen's mate. Where is she? Is she all right?"

"I'm on my way to her now. I put a tracker in her phone."

"Oh, thank Fate."

"Do you know what she's planning?"

"I suspect she's trying to draw Dirk away from you and the Denver pack. She didn't want anyone to get hurt because of her."

"*She's* trying to protect *me*." I curse, gunning the vehicle forward, racing far above the speed limit.

"Dirk's a real piece of work, Mark. He told everyone your pack kidnapped her. It would've been better if she'd let you mark her, but she was afraid he'd tear you both to pieces if that happened."

I bare my teeth, a savage growl ripping from my throat. My mate had to live with this psychopath. "I'm going to tear him to pieces if he even touches her," I vow.

"Be careful. Please keep me posted?"

"Yeah." I end the call.

Colleen. My chest constricts tightly. She hadn't been unsure of me. She'd been protecting me. My foolish little mate. Doesn't she know I'd rather die than ever let her get hurt again?

COLLEEN

My palms sweat as I sit on the concrete bench near the lake to wait.

I texted Dirk when I got here and added my dad to the thread to make sure there was a witness. *Your story about me being kidnapped by the Denver pack is ludicrous. I left you because I refuse to allow me or our pups to be your punching bag any longer. Tell your pack to turn around and go home.*

He must've been too angry to notice my dad was on the thread, or maybe he didn't care any more because he responded, *I will kill you all.*

My heart pounded as I texted, *Leave the Denver pack out of it. I am not with them.*

I will find you.

Lave the Denver pack alone. I'll meet you at Evergreen Lake.

Neither he nor my father replied after that, but I'm certain Dirk's on his way. So I wait, trying not to think about Mark and how upset he'll be when he discovers what I've done. Or the pups and what might happen to them if I don't succeed. Instead, I focus on my breath. In. Out. Steady. Fate's on my side. She brought me to my mate. Now all I have to do is finish this.

I know the moment he arrives. The hairs on the back of my neck stand up, and my skin prickles with goosebumps as the unfamiliar car—no doubt a rental—pulls into the parking area. I reach back instinctively and touch the pistol in my waistband.

He gets out and slams the door before storming toward me.

I don't stand. I just wait for him to stalk my way. Even across the field I read the anger radiating from him, his violence close to the surface, prepped to deliver. Of course, it triggers me. Adrenaline flushes my system so fast I nearly shift to run into the woods. But I already know how that scenario goes. He'd catch me, and I'd suffer for it.

No, this time I'm not going to run. I'm going to fight back.

So I get up and walk toward him, chin lifted high, my molars clenched. I pull the gun when he's five feet away and point it at him. My hand trembles, but that doesn't stop me from taking off the safety. "You get any closer, and I'll kill you," I tell him.

He sneers. "You think a gun will stop me?" He lunges for me.

I shoot. Dirk's body jerks with the impact.

I register the arrival of two more cars in the parking lot and the attention I've drawn with the gunshot.

Fuck. Witnesses.

And double-fuck. My aim was off.

The bullet caught him in the shoulder, not the

heart. He staggers back, eyes turning amber, lips peeling back in a snarl. "Silver." He recognizes the damaging properties of the only substance that can harm shifters.

He closes the distance between us.

I freeze for a moment, that old familiar terror rising in me.

It gives him the advantage he requires. He tries to grab the pistol. I yank my hand back, firing into the air, but then he knocks it from my hand. I dive for it, but he grips my skull, arms cocked to snap my neck.

I hear the snarl of a wolf at the same time a shot rings out.

Dirk crumples to the ground, dead.

My knees buckle, and I almost fall, too, but the great black wolf barrelling toward me seamlessly shifts into human form, and Mark catches me and lifts me into his arms.

I stare at Dirk on the ground in confusion. "How... who..."

And then I see my father, jogging toward us, a gun in his hand. "Colleen!" There's fear in his voice.

Mark holds me closer as if to protect me from him, too. I wrap my arms around his neck in a strangle-hold, breathing in my mate's intoxicating scent. "I'm sorry. I'm so sorry."

"He almost killed you." My dad sounds shocked.

Mark ignores him. "Fuck, baby. Fuck. I'm so glad you're all right."

"I'm all right. Where are my pups?" My head snaps toward the parking lot, hoping Mark didn't bring them.

"A family from the pack took them until things blow over."

My father stands behind Mark, and for the first time in my life, he appears unsure of himself. Awkward, even. "Colleen. I'm sorry, Co-co," he says, calling me by my childhood nickname. He runs his hand through his salt and pepper hair. "I'm so sorry. Why didn't you tell me how bad it was?"

Mark seems reluctant to put me down, but after a moment's pause, he does. Still, he keeps me tucked closely into his side, standing with his clothes in tatters around his large, muscled body.

"He said he'd kill you if you ever challenged him," I admit. "He said he'd destroy your whole pack. I couldn't have that on my conscience."

My dad swears. "Dirk was bad news, and I should've seen it. I'm so goddamn sorry."

For the first time, I steal a look at Dirk's body. "You killed him." My father shot him straight through the head, which will kill a shifter, even without silver bullets.

"I sure as hell did." He clears his throat. "And you are?" he says to Mark.

"Oh! Dad, this is Mark, my true mate. Mark, my father, Aaron Blackthorn."

Mark waits a few beats before extending his hand to my dad. He doesn't say *nice to meet you* or *how do you do*? He probably blames my dad for saddling me with Dirk.

My dad grips it and bows his head, receiving Mark's unspoken judgement.

"I'll take care of this." Mark eyes Dirk's fallen body distastefully. "You take Colleen back to my place."

My father's not used to being ordered around, but he accepts the directive with a nod. "You sure you've got this?"

"Yes. I'm an enforcer."

My dad's brows flick like he's impressed, not that I care. I'm long past living the life he wanted for me.

"Can you handle his pack?" Mark asks my dad.

"Yes. I created this problem. I'll fix it."

Mark lifts his chin at Dirk's body. "Honestly, I'm glad it was you. I didn't want to have to be the one who killed the pup's father, and I didn't want that for Colleen, either." He wraps his hand around my nape and pulls my head closer to press a kiss to my forehead.

"Jayden and Angie won't cry over his death," I

say quietly, which makes both Mark and my dad scowl.

"Go on—I've got this," Mark promises.

I wrap my arms around him and squeeze tightly as my dad walks back to the car. "Thank you. I'm sorry. Are you mad?" I whisper.

"Not mad. Just so fucking relieved." He holds me, rocking from foot to foot like we're slow dancing.

I press myself close again, needing to feel him, dying to get skin-to-skin. "I'm ready for you to mark me."

Mark pulls back, and I see corners of his lips quirk as his eyes change to silver. "Oh, I'm going to mark you, sweetheart. I'm going to make sure you never forget who you belong to." He touches my nose. "And there will definitely be consequences for this, babygirl."

I lift on my tiptoes to kiss his neck. "I love you."

Mark's arm bands around me, and his lips crash down on mine as he lifts me to straddle his waist. "I love you so much, Colleen." I feel the thunder of his heart against my chest. His mouth twists over mine, angles one way, then the other, as he carries me toward the parking lot.

"Now be a good girl and go home—to *our* home. I need to know you're safe, and I can't focus on cleaning this up until I'm sure." He walks me straight to the passenger side of the car my dad's sitting in and lowers me to my feet.

"Okay." I kiss him this time. "I'll be waiting."

"You'd *better* be." There's a levity to his tone that lifts the heaviness of everything that just happened.

I'm with Mark now. My true mate.

Everything's going to be all right.

6

Mark

Colleen waits on my bed—no, *our* bed—wearing one of my t-shirts.

It's late—her father took the pups to stay with him at a hotel for the night—correctly intuiting that we could use some alone-time to resolve things between us. He bribed them with the promise of ordering room service and swimming in the pool, so they were content enough to go, despite the stress of their day.

I spent the afternoon taking care of Dirk's body, making it look like he was trafficking drugs and was the victim of a drug gang execution and then meeting with Ben, my alpha, Colleen's dad, and the Lexington pack to resolve things once and for all.

Now, freshly out of the shower, my blood sings in anticipation of marking my female.

She seems completely changed now that the threat of Dirk has been removed. Her wariness is gone. Where I could tell she was holding back before, she now seems open and receptive. Mine.

"Clothes off, baby," I command when I find her sitting on her heels in the center of the bed. She looks so submissive waiting for me, her attentive gaze on my face.

She whips the shirt off and tosses it to the floor, and I discover she was wearing nothing underneath.

A growl of approval crawls up my throat as I stalk closer. "Oh, sweet girl. That is so beautiful."

Her nipples bead up, eyes change to amber. I scent her arousal.

"Little wolf, you upset me today," I tell her in a mock-stern voice.

"I know, Daddy. I'm sorry."

"I was so scared for you." I gently position her on her knees, then push her torso down until her ass is in the air. "I thought I might lose you."

"I know."

I run my hand over the curve of her ass, stroking her. "You were trying to protect me by not letting me mark you, weren't you?"

"I was just scared," she says, and my heart squeezes.

"Please don't ever push me out of the picture again." I deliver a slap to her ass. "If you're in trouble, I want to be there beside you." I slap the other cheek.

"Yes, Daddy."

"Are you going to let me take care of you?" I spank her again.

"Yes! Yes, please."

I chuckle because she's so damn sweet. I could never really punish her, especially not with what she's been through. She needs to always know she's safe with me.

"Give me this ass." I grip both cheeks and pull them apart, rimming her asshole with my tongue.

"Oh!" She squeals, her anus fluttering against my tongue.

"I'm going to fuck you here tonight. That's what happens when you're naughty."

The sweet smell of her arousal tells me she's perfectly on board with that idea.

I rub two fingers between her legs, finding her clit and tapping it a few times before I deliver a little spank.

"First I'm going to spank this sweet pussy, and then I'm going to get my dick wet, just enough to draw my teeth down. And then I'm going to mark your sweet little ass as mine forever."

Colleen moans her assent as I rub a light circle around her clit.

I spank her pussy with quick light slaps, reveling

in the way her juices run over my fingers each time I make contact.

I don't even need to dip my cock inside her—I'm already hard as stone with my fangs down, ripe with the serum that leaves my scent forever embedded in her flesh.

But I'm a male of my word. I spank her pussy until her moans turn desperate and wanton, then I spear her with my erection, driving in so deep she cries out with pleasure.

"Yes, Daddy!"

"That's it, babygirl. Take my cock," I growl, pulling back, then slamming in again.

"Yes, please. I want it. I want it so badly," she begs.

Fuck.

I pump in with shorter strokes, bumping her ass each time, making my balls draw up tight like I'm already ready to go off. But I won't. I have other plans tonight. I grip her hips to make it satisfying for both of us, deep and firm. My balls slap against her clit. My thumb pushes against her back entrance.

Just when I'm sure she's about to come—when her walls start to squeeze and her moans turn into desperate cries—I pull out and sink my fangs into her beautiful ass.

She screams and bucks as if the pain gives her

as much pleasure as the fucking. I breach her hole, and I hold her like that, captive to my bite, my thumb opening her for what comes next.

She comes, moaning and begging, her fingers seeking her clit between her legs.

It takes me a moment to regain my humanity, but the satisfaction of having marked her is the most intoxicating high I've ever been on. I withdraw my thumb and fangs and lick the wound closed as Colleen continues to work her fingers between her legs, moaning.

"I'm sorry, babygirl. Did I leave you empty when you came?"

"Yes, Daddy."

"Don't worry, I'm about to stuff you full of my cock, sweetheart. Don't move." I leave her for a moment to grab the lubricant I picked up on my way home. Using a generous amount, I coat my cock and her anus, then arrange a pillow under her hips to make her more comfortable.

I pepper her ass with a few more spanks. "Reach back and open your ass for me," I command.

She immediately obeys, obviously completely trusting of me at this point.

I straddle her hips and rub the head of my cock over her anus. "Take me."

She squeezes at first, but I wait until her anus

relaxes and opens. I ease forward, going slowly as she gets used to having her ass filled.

"Good girl," I praise, and she relaxes more. "Put your fingers between your legs again, sweet-heart. Work that pussy for me while I fuck your ass."

"Yes, Daddy."

I fucking love how agreeable she is. How on board. How willingly she goes with my dirty talk and kinky play.

Once I'm all the way inside her, I start to pump slowly. Just a little. In and out. Gradually I let the movements grow until I'm stroking all the way—filling and emptying her.

Her moans and the slick sounds of frantic fingers working between her legs fill the room.

"Are you going to put yourself in danger again, babygirl?"

"No, Daddy!"

"No. You're going to let your daddy take care of you, aren't you?"

"Yes. Yes, please. I need that." She sounds desperate, like she's going to come again.

It makes me desperate to orgasm as well.

"Fuck," I growl, pumping faster, trying not to let my movements get erratic or jerky as my thighs tense.

"Please, please, Daddy!" she squeals.

I shout and shove in deep, filling her ass with my cum as I reach around the front of her hips to sink my fingers deep in her squeezing cunt.

"Oh Fates, yes," I pant against her ear, rocking slowly.

"Yes," she moans her agreement.

"You're mine now," I tell her, panting against her back. I kiss her ear, her jaw, along her hairline.

"You're mine," she says back. "I'm going to take care of you, too."

I chuckle and ease out of her. "Stay there, baby-girl," I murmur, then get up to bring a washcloth and clean her up. When I finish she rolls over, and I pull the pillow out and settle on top of her, dropping kisses all over her lovely heart-shaped face.

"You don't need to take care of me, little wolf. Having you in my bed is reward enough. I want you to take care of yourself. You could go to college if you wanted. Or stay home. Or work. Anything that lights you up. That's what I want from you."

She wraps her arms and legs around me, yanking me flush against her.

I chuckle. "I'm going to squish you, sweetheart."

"No you won't," she says, face buried in my neck.

"I love you, sweet girl."

"You're more than my mate. More than my

daddy. You're a hero, in the true sense of the word. You give yourself for the protection of others. Travis would be honored with what you've done in his memory, and I'm so proud to be your mate."

My eyes and nose get hot for a moment. "Thank you, babygirl."

EPILOGUE

Colleen

"I hear the heartbeat," Mark murmurs, his ear pressed to my swollen belly.

We're on our babymoon—the honeymoon you take *before* the baby arrives, since afterward there will be no sleep—in a cabin in the Swiss Alps. The pups are staying with a shifter family in Denver who have kids almost the exact same ages. I talked to them on the phone this morning, and they sounded like they were having the time of their lives.

I giggle. "Even with shifter hearing, you can't possibly hear her heartbeat."

Mark lifts his head and grins. "*Her?* Do you know something you're not sharing?"

I flush. "I've been having dreams."

"Oh yeah?" He strokes a circle around my belly, then over my hip. "What did you dream, babygirl?"

"I dreamt we had her in a cabin like this one—but in Colorado. The pups were there, and you caught her. You held her in your hands and called out, *It's a girl,* and all four of us started crying with joy."

Mark's eyes get misty, the same way they had in my dream. "Sounds perfect."

He's been an amazing father to Angie and Jayden. They adore him. Having an asshole for a father made them completely open and grateful for a father who is kind and attentive. Honorable.

They both did well in the human school I put them in, and I enrolled in community college although I still haven't decided what I want to major in. I was planning to drop out when the baby comes, but Mark said I should try to stay in school and just take one class at a time. I think he wants me to know I have more options than staying home, raising pups and serving my mate.

But with him, it's never like that. He dotes on me. Takes care of us. All he wants in return is *me*. Which I can happily give.

He gave up his role as enforcer for the shifter council, and I don't worry about him too much working for the DEA, since he's mostly bullet-proof.

I push up to my hands and knees and climb over him. Even though we just had sex a half an hour ago, I'm already needy for more. This pregnancy has me horny all hours of the day. Mark's eyes glint silver with satisfaction, and he grips my hips, tugging me over his erection. "You look so beautiful."

I cup my enlarged breasts and let out a husky laugh. This pregnancy has been easy. I feel beautiful —probably because Mark tells me I am five times a day. I start to rock over Mark's cock, taking him deeper, then easing back. It feels so good, but then, it always feels good. I went from nightmare to dream life almost overnight.

I drop my hands to his shoulders, so I can work my hips faster. My hair, which has grown long and thick, trails against his neck. "I'm so happy I found my Daddy," I purr.

His eyes crinkle even though I can see his need mounting in the silver of his irises. "Best day of my life," he agrees. He grips my hips and takes over the work, pulling me over his cock, controlling our rhythm. I toss my head back, arching into the pleasure as he makes me ride him faster and faster, winding the spring up tight before he brings his thumb to my clit and rubs. "Come all over Daddy's cock," he commands.

"Yes, Daddy!" My muscles seize around his dick, squeezing and milking it as pleasure rockets through me from my core out in all directions.

Mark shouts and spears me, lifting his hips off the bed, suspending both our bodies in the air as he fills me with his seed. "That's it, babygirl." He drops back down to the bed, still inside me. "Good girl." He pulls my hips over his dick slowly, wringing more little earthquakes from me until I collapse over him in exhaustion.

"Naptime," he murmurs as my eyes flutter closed. His arms band around me, holding me tight.

"Mmm. Thank you, Daddy."

He chuckles softly. "You don't have to thank me for sex, babygirl. Pleasuring you is my job."

I nuzzle my face into his neck, breathing in his leather and coffee scent. "I love you."

He eases us to our sides because the position isn't sustainable with my big belly between us. "I'm crazy for you, angel. You and our pups are all I live for."

"Same," I murmur as a well-earned sleep takes over, and I drift into dreamland again.

BIO:

***USA Today* Bestselling Author Renee Rose** loves a dominant, dirty-talking alpha hero! She's sold over a million copies of steamy romance with varying levels of kink. Her books have been featured in *USA Today's Happily Ever After* and *Popsugar*. Named *Eroticon USA's Next Top Erotic Author* in 2013, she has also won *Spunky and Sassy's* Favorite

Sci-Fi and Anthology author, and *Romance Reviews* Best Historical Romance. She's hit the *USA Today* list nine times with her Chicago Bratva, Bad Boy Alpha, Wolf Ranch books, and various anthologies.

GET A RENEE ROSE BOOKS HERE: https://subscribepage.com/alphastemp

SHE CAN BE FOUND ON:

FACEBOOK: https://facebook.com/reneeroseromance

Amazon: https://geni.us/reneerose

Website: www.reneeroseromance.com

WANT MORE?

READ NOW —>

Wolf Ranch Book 1 - Rough

Pack Rule #1: Never reveal to a human.

I broke that rule the day I met the beautiful doctor.

WANT FREE RENEE ROSE BOOKS?

Go to http://subscribepage.-com/alphastemp to sign up for Renee Rose's newsletter and receive a free copy of *Alpha's Tempta-*

tion, Theirs to Protect, Owned by the Marine, Theirs to Punish, The Alpha's Punishment, Disobedience at the Dressmaker's and *Her Billionaire Boss.* In addition to the free stories, you will also get special pricing, exclusive previews and news of new releases.

OTHER TITLES BY RENEE ROSE

Paranormal

Wolf Ridge High Series

Alpha Bully

Alpha Knight

Step Alpha

Alpha King

Bad Boy Alphas Series

Alpha's Temptation

Alpha's Danger

Alpha's Prize

Alpha's Challenge

Alpha's Obsession

Alpha's Desire

Alpha's War

Alpha's Mission

Alpha's Bane

Alpha's Secret

Alpha's Prey

Alpha's Sun

Zandian Masters Series

His Human Slave

His Human Prisoner

Training His Human

His Human Rebel

His Human Vessel

His Mate and Master

Zandian Pet

Their Zandian Mate

His Human Possession

Zandian Brides

Night of the Zandians

Bought by the Zandians

Mastered by the Zandians

Zandian Lights

Kept by the Zandian

Claimed by the Zandian

Stolen by the Zandian

Rescued by the Zandian

Other Sci-Fi

The Hand of Vengeance

Her Alien Masters

ABOUT RENEE ROSE

USA TODAY BESTSELLING AUTHOR RENEE ROSE loves a dominant, dirty-talking alpha hero! She's sold over two million copies of steamy romance with varying levels of kink. Her books have been featured in USA Today's *Happily Ever After* and *Popsugar*. Named Eroticon USA's Next Top Erotic Author in 2013, she has also won *Spunky and Sassy's* Favorite Sci-Fi and Anthology author, *The Romance Reviews* Best Historical Romance, and has hit the *USA Today* list fifteen times with her Bad Boy Alphas, Chicago Bratva, and Wolf Ranch series.

Renee loves to connect with readers!
www.reneeroseromance.com
reneeroseauthor@gmail.com

facebook.com/reneeroseromance

instagram.com/reneeroseromance

bookbub.com/authors/renee-rose